HERBERT E. BAZRON

HEALING FLURRIES

AF565680

Healing Flurries

Herbert E. Bazron

Copyright © 2024 **Baz Bliss Ink Publishing**

All rights reserved. No part of this publication may be reproduced, distributed, or transmitted in any form or by any means, including photocopying, recording, or other electronic or mechanical methods, without the prior written permission of the publisher, except in the case of brief quotations embodied in critical reviews and certain other noncommercial uses permitted by copyright law. For permission requests, write to the publisher, addressed "Attention: Book Rights and Permission," at the address below.

Published in the United States of America

ISBN 979-8-89395-874-4 (SC)
ISBN 979-8-89395-873-7 (Ebook)

Baz Bliss Ink Publishing
222 West 6th Street
Suite 400, San Pedro, CA, 90731
www.stellarliterary.com

Order Information and Rights Permission:

Quantity sales. Special discounts might be available on quantity purchases by corporations, associations, and others. For details, contact the publisher at the address above.

For Book Rights Adaptation and other Rights Permission. Call us at toll-free 1-888-945-8513 or send us an email at admin@stellarliterary.com

Contents

Chapter 1

Harper Sun mashes her foot on the gas as she weaves down a windy two-way road headed for home. The temperature outside is dropping. She has half a tank of gas, and her check engine light is illuminated. Her music—the dance mix version of "Driver's License" by Olivia Rodrigo—is blaring. The beat's bass is pounding the windows, drowning out everything except Harper's sorrows.

Her phone continuously lights up with alerts of the upcoming winter storm set to blanket the Northern Territory. This type of weather is very common for Northern Canada, this storm marking the third one of the seasons. However, there is something different about this barreling storm. Harper feels this is so because she wishes for something different from how her life has been the last couple of years. She has been in a fragile state of mind, on the verge of ending it all. Even though her selfish, asshole ex-husband jumped ship, she did not expect to be alone in such a vulnerable time. Thus, her good spirits and joy for life have been obliterated. She is almost soulless.

She steps on the gas harder and turns the music up even louder; she screams along with the song. She is exercising a "ZFG" attitude in getting to her property. She has no regard for the killer winter storm coming.

Meanwhile, above the tundra, a large utility helicopter whips through the graying, frigid, turbulent air. As the conditions are deteriorating, so is the hydraulic system of the aged helicopter carrying seven souls. One soul is Fela Zamore, nicknamed 2Z. He is the CEO and cofounder of a video game software company. He is on his first trip to Canada, a Northern Territory adventure tour. It has been a much-needed getaway from the daily chaos of Atlanta. Fela has been trying to find some remedy for his anxiety and prejudice. He took this wilderness exploration trip to see different faces. He is a hard charger. He and his partners laid the roots of their multimillion- dollar software company against the backdrop of tragedy.

Fela has experienced a lot in only thirty-two years of life. Fela experienced the horror of death caused by racial bias as a teenager. Watching a friend die in front of him forged animosity and venom in him. He knows the dominant destructive trait in his character is his prejudice toward the white race—white women specifically— that makes him fear merely being in their presence. So, this trip was supposed to support positive interactions with the diverse tourist group. However, one member, named Barry, has prevented this healing; he has engaged in incendiary, divisive political rants as well as racially charged dog whistling.

Now, the pilots, Joey and Jac, struggle with the stick to maintain control of the helicopter. It is no use. All the while, the bird is dropping rapidly as alarms blare. The two very experienced pilots start issuing, "Mayday," on the open channels. Fela and his fellow passengers, Ula, Chandler, Barry, and Jun are all gripped by fear. Jac makes a very unconvincing attempt to calm the passengers, but he knows the bird is going down.

The barrage of snow intensifies as the helicopter is getting closer and closer to the white landscape. Chandler begins to pray out loud over everyone for them to survive the impending crash. Jun and Barr y reach for hysterical Ula's hands to comfort her. Fela tucks his chin to his chest and makes himself into a ball to brace for impact. He has no interest in cuddling anyone's hand for comfort, especially Barr y's, as he believes that this is the end.

Twenty-five seconds—what seems like minutes—later, the first hard thud of hitting the ground occurs. Then, as the helicopter bounces upward, blasts of white snow fill the helicopter as it violently rolls. Screams of fear and pain and sounds of crumpling metal ring out as the remaining pieces of the helicopter spin in the snow. Finally, after forty seconds have passed, the mangled frame of the helicopter comes to a stop. A nearly mile- long trail of scattered debris lies across the tundra. The wind shrieks.

There's an eerie silence as radio chatter is heard but can't be made out. Someone moans and says, "Oh Jesus," but otherwise, it's coldly quiet. Fela comes to and is immediately jolted with pain from his back. He has a laceration across his forehead, and there is a piece of metal impaled in his right calf. He is alive but very disoriented.

He scans the wreckage, looking to see what is. Barry yells, “Who is alive?” Jun answers along with Joey.

What’s left of the helicopter’s frame is horrifying, looking like it was battered with anti-aircraft artillery. The survivors begin to struggle to exit the wreckage. They are minus two: Chandler and Ula. It appears they were ejected from the helicopter in its violent rolling across the tundra. Joey pleads for some help as Barry starts to squirm and crawl. He is a bloody mess, but for the most part can function; he is a big guy at six foot four, and hard charging.

Jun looks at Fela and sees his badly injured right leg. “Hang on, friend,” he calmly tells Fela. Jun is laboring due to his hurt right shoulder and his head injury but, without hesitation, is willing to provide aid. Fela is in pain but pridefully says, “I’m good, Jun,” as he squirms in agony out of the helicopter and into the brutal cold. Jun is persistent in assisting Fela. “Please, friend, let’s help each other,” he says as they eye a wooded area. The two stagger and drag each other toward some kind of cover from the ever-increasing blanketing snow.

Barry gets to Joey and, unaware of his own injuries, lifts the badly injured pilot. As they peer down at the lifeless body of Jac, Joey wails with tears. Barry tries to calm Joey as he is hauling him from the wreckage, fearing explosion at any minute, as sparks and fuel secrete from the fuselage of the mangled wreck.

Jun yells out and flicks a flashlight to direct Barry to the tree line. Barry hustles to this rallying point, gently laying Joey on the ground. Here, the men brainstorm what is the best course of action to get to shelter. Joey has familiarity with the area normally but is very disoriented from the crash. The other men try to maintain their composure so they can get out of this dangerous ordeal they are facing.

Barry steps up. “I’ll take charge to get us out of this,” he says as he dives into his alpha-male mentality. He leans down to Joey and inquires as to their handheld GPS’s operating condition to navigate by foot. The GPS seems to be damaged to the point of questionable accuracy. Plus, Jun, Fela, and Joey cannot walk with their injuries. Barry gets the idea to go back to the wreckage and utilize one of the helicopter doors as a makeshift sled to pull them. Immediately, as he makes his first step, kaboom! The ravaged remains of the helicopter burst into flames.

Barry immediately turns to the group with a flustered look but seems determined to find a solution. Hands on his hips, he says, “Now what?” knowing things are getting dire.

Meanwhile, about fifteen miles south of the stranded men’s position lies a cozy two-story cabin on three acres of land, being blasted with snow. However, it is sturdy against the harsh Canadian winter climate. Inside the cabin, music is blaring, coffee is brewing, and darts are f lying. Harper is blowing off steam by flinging darts at a board with a man’s face in the center. The face is that of her ex-husband, who abandoned her in a very vulnerable time.

After quite a few shots of whiskey, Harper tries to compose herself. Her eyes are puffy, her pupils red, indicating that she has been crying for some time. Her arm and shoulder muscles are failing, trembling from constant push-ups between dart flingings. Her chest looks pumped up like inflated airbags, as she is a f it, athletic, and voluptuous woman. She played basketball and soccer, ran track, and did CrossFit throughout high school. She has been burdened with a lot, which has left her battle hardened.

To cool off and sober up, Harper pours herself a cup of coffee. Suddenly, there is a banging at her front door, with some urgent yells of her name. She places the coffee on the counter and moves to the door. She f lings it open with a bit of irritation when she sees Jimo, her nearest neighbor, who lives less than a mile away. He is frantic.

Harper ushers Jimo out of the elements and attempts to calm him down to see what the emergency is. Why the hell is he out in this blizzard? She wants to get him to speak on the situation with some clarity.

Harper: Jimo, what the hell. … What's going on?

Jimo (*shaking*): Harper, look, I'm sorry, and it seems you may not be totally prepared for this, but … Jesus, Harper, a helicopter went down maybe fifteen miles north of us.

Harper (*clutching her face*): Oh my God, your serious right now? How?

Jimo: Yes! We heard a faint Mayday on the radio while frequency hopping. Harper, we need your help, like right now! Two of my brothers and his friends are right behind me pulling some sleds. We must help; can you grab your medic bag?

Harper: Jimo, how can you find the site? It's white out, the wind gust is heavy, and the temperatures are dropping by the minute to the extremes. Did you contact the rescue services? There is not too much we can do but put ourselves in danger. How do you know if there are even any survivors?

Jimo: It's no time for those questions. Please, we just must try to help; we still have enough visibility to navigate to the site. If emergency services are there, that's great. However, it was by God that I heard the transmission of the Mayday. My gut says that maybe the emergency services did not get this message, or even worse, this storm is going to delay them. We are closer.

Harper *(skeptically)*: Okay, okay … let me bundle up as much as I can and get my bag. Go to my shed around back. I have a spinal board. Can you transport that?

Jimo: Whatever you need to assist us.

Harper: Thank you, and can you start my snowmobile? Just give me about ten minutes, and we can depart.

As the group prepares to move out, the odds are gravely stacking up against the four men back at the crash site. The men are starting to grow a bit frustrated as they try to come up with a plan. Well, at most, Barry is trying to come up with something and not hearing anyone else's input. Joey is concussed and unable to be any help to the cause. So, this is fueling Barry to hard-charge and dismiss Jun's and Fela's concerns.

Barry takes Joey in a fireman's carry and begins walking due south. He gives very little consideration to whether Fela or Jun can keep up with his pace. Despite his injuries, Fela immediately voices his displeasure at Barry's bullheaded decision making. As Jun tries to calm Fela, he assists him in limping along in the snow.

Fela: This is absurd! How the hell do you know the way to some safety and shelter, Barry?

Jun: Fela!

Fela: No, Jun, this is bullshit!

Barry: Mr. Z, can you lead us out in your condition? Do you know where we are going? Do you know, Jun?

Jun: No! But that's why we put our heads together and figure it out, instead of you just thinking in everyone's best interest, Barry.

Barry: We are moving out. You can protest and moan as we try to make it to shelter. That seems like minority protesting to me because I'm leading in front, as it should be, guys. Start walking or stay and parish; your fates are not a footnote to me.

Chapter 2

Twenty minutes have passed. Harper and crew are pushing through the whiteness with their snowmobiles at full throttle, navigating only on gut instinct and the will to help. However, they won't be able to go too much longer, as the will of the storm is growing stronger. The snow on the ground is thick, and the storm is brutal. Despite the layers of clothing, they are really getting colder and colder each mile.

This scenario could evolve to where the rescuers will need to be rescued. Harper is realizing this as the whiskey, which impaired her judgment to embark on a less-than-coordinated rescue mission, is wearing off. As she suddenly brings her snowmobile to a stop, she yells at the top of her lungs and flickers her flashlight. This gets the attention of the other two, who stop their snowmobiles and corral them around Harper.

Harper: *(yelling)*: Hey, this is getting worse! These people could be anywhere!

Jimo: Come on, just a little further!

Harper: Jimo … no, I'm not going any further. We are putting ourselves in just as much danger.

Jimo: Harp!

Harper: No!

Spen: Hey, guys, I see, like, a faint spot of light to my three o'clock. Seriously!

Jimo: Are you sure?

Spen: I see something or someone. Give me a flare! Come on!

Jimo hands a flare to Spen, who points straight above his head and fires, hoping it's enough light for anyone out there to see. Spen is realizing that Harper has had enough, and he himself is realizing that this was a bad idea. However, about a mile away, Barry has seen the faint flare.

Barry is exhausted from carrying Joey for what seems like miles on pure adrenaline, while Jun has been like a human crutch for Fela. Barry has a flare gun, which he fires up in the air, hoping it will be seen.

Spen: My God … there is a flare. I think we found them.

Jimo: All right, let's roll. You ready, Harper?

Harper: Let's get them so we can get the hell out of this storm.

Barry: I hear something! Sounds like snowmobiles. Let's go, guys!

The men proceed up a small embankment as Barry flashes a flashlight, hoping it is spotted. Jimo gets visual confirmation of the men's location. Jimo, Harper, and Spen pull up. Realizing they don't want to f lip their sled, they dismount the snowmobiles and proceed on foot to the edge, where they greet the four men.

Barry: Some help, please!

Jimo: Hang on.

Spen: Give me your hand, sir.

Harper: Okay, let's assess this here. Who is the most badly injured? We'll get them on the sled first.

Barry: Here! Joey—he is the surviving pilot, and he is in bad shape. I don't know how serious the other two men's conditions are. They have been bitching mostly the whole track. Isn't that something? They always do, don't they, Hoss?

Jun: What the hell! We are both injured and need some medical attention—my friend more than me. He has a leg injury and a gash on his head. We'll speak for ourselves. Please, a little help.

Fela (*extremely annoyed*): I'll speak for me, Jun. I am coherent enough.

Barry (*angrily disappointed*): Wait … there is just three of you? You're not an official rescue team? Emergency services?

Harper: Sir, we are here to help you, we are well equipped, and I have trauma expertise. Right now, with this storm you're in, no helicopters or ambulances will be dispatched. Sensible people are sheltered in place. We are all you guys have right now for survival; we have shelter and other essentials. Now that you know this, we must go now!

Jimo: She is right.

Spen: Wait … Barry, right? How did y'all end up out here? Your part of a tourist adventure excursion, aren't you? So foolish. All the tour consultants were warned seventy-two hours ago of the storm impacting the area.

Barry: Great … good to know now. How far away are we from the nearest hospital?

Jimo: From where we are, no more than thirty miles to Yellowknife. With this storm, however, we might as well be 250 miles away. The main roads are inaccessible. Does that answer everything?

Barry: Fine. Me and Joey are ready. We need care and shelter.

Harper: Why do you keep overlooking the other two of your party?

Fela: I don't need a damn thing from anybody (*pointing at Barry*), especially this blatherskite bigot!

Barry: Screw you, guy! It's always the same nonsense with people like you.

Fela (*irately pushing aside Jun*): What!

Fela tries to charge Barry, but his leg injury causes him to lose his footing. He falls backward, down the small embankment in the thick snow. He comes to a stop at the bottom and blacks out.

Harper: Oh God! Get these three out of here. Jimo, help me get this guy up.

Jun: His name is Fela.

Harper: Okay, help me with Fela, Jimo.

Jun: I'm fine. I want to help.

Harper: No, please … go, Jun. He is in good hands; y'all get to shelter. Please go!

Barry: Great, it's settled. … Leaving his black ass in white snow would do him some good.

Harper *(turning back, appalled)*: Thank you for your unnecessary and vile input, Barry. You can go now. Best of luck to you, sir.

Barry *(turning back to Harper)*: Jeez, whose side are you on, little snow lady?

Harper: I'm on the side of humanity and being a decent person, Hoss!

Fela opens his eyes for a moment of coherence. He sees Harper and Jimo talking over him for a few seconds. He drifts off again, then opens his eyes, looking up at nothing but white flurries.

Along with the sensation of bouncing up and down every ten seconds, his head is pounding, and the sensation is making his leg pain unbearable. He is screaming, but he can't hear himself over the noise of the revving snowmobiles. He closes his eyes again, for a much longer period.

Twenty-four hours later, the storm has ended, leaving more than ten inches of snow on the ground. The sun is starting to peak out; it's 9:18 in the morning. Fela is starting to fully awaken. As he tries to look around at the cabin, his neck is sore. His head is bandaged, his leg is braced, and his ankle is wrapped very tight. He slowly sits up on the modified sofa bed that he has been on since arriving to this cabin. He doesn't know whose cabin he is in. Where is the host?

He does not have to wonder long as someone comes down the stairs. Glancing over at him with a smile, Harper is elated to see that he is up and coherent. Fela is taken aback by her ethnicity. He gazes displeasingly at her as she makes her way to him to greet him.

Harper: Hey, good morning.

Fela *(with a standoffish pause)*: Um … good morning.

Harper (*still smiling*): How do you feel?

Fela: Look at me. How do you think I feel?

Harper (*unfazed*): Okay … I guess I can understand that.

Fela: Who are you? Who did all this bandaging and bracing?

Harper: Me … Harper Sun.

Fela: You're a doctor … Mrs. Sun?

Harper: I was an ER trauma nurse. And I'm not married. Please call me Harper. What is your name again? I heard it briefly from your expedition party members.

Fela: Fela Zamore. My friends and the media just call me 2Z.

Harper: 2Z? That's unique. So, do you have a big sister named 1Z? I'm sorry, I couldn't help myself.

Fela: Really? I've heard that before quite a few times. So, is that a problem?

Harper: No … sir, not at all. What would you like me to call you?

Fela: Whatever is comfortable for you. Just don't call me out of my name. I deal with enough of that down south still, believe it or not.

Harper *(a little perplexed)*: Okay, I understand, 2Z.

Fela: Normally, friends call me 2Z. But you did help me, so I'm cool with it. So, what is the status? Are emergency services on the way to come get me? Is that the rescue plan?

Harper: I was the plan. You were rescued from certain death. The storm has passed, but roads are still impassable, and rescue is reserved for critical emergency priorities. You are stable, sheltered, and have medical care.

Fela: What? I understand, but this is not a hospital, Ms. Sun. I don't dismiss your medical expertise in first aid. However, what if things are worse than what you've seen? My head, ankle, calf, and my back now. You expect to keep me here? Have I been here for about twenty-four hours or so?

Harper: Yes, you have, but let me be straight with you. It'll probably be two more days until I get you to town. I'm going to need you to have some patience here with me, 2Z. I understand you probably don't want to be here, but you are safe and in good care.

Fela (*visibly irritated)*: No! What do you need? How much to charter some transportation? Ten thousand? Twenty thousand? How much do I need to give you to get out of here?

Harper: *(shaking her he*ad): Your wallet is not going to get you out of here faster. You can't throw dollars at nature, 2Z. It'll throw them back and kill you where you stand. You are fine. … I'll get you to Yellowknife in about forty- eight hours.

Fela: Great! Ms. Sun, I am an executive. People are going to look for me. My personal assistant is expecting me back Saturday in Atlanta. Where is my phone?

Harper: You're an executive of what?

Fela: I'm a CEO of a video game software and development company. I'm an entrepreneur, and a new shareholder in a professional wrestling territory.

Harper: Oh, wow, what is the name of the wrestling federation? I watch wrestling.

Fela: I don't want to be rude here, but can I get my stuff to make a call?

Harper: Oh, okay, sure. I put all your loose belongings in the wicker basket on the table—your wallet, sunglasses, and a bracelet that I secured for you.

Fela: My phone was not on me or in the area where you found me?

Harper: No, I'm sorry, it wasn't, 2Z. Look, my cell can make calls to the United States. You're welcome to call who you need so they know what has happened.

Fela (*palming his face*): That's not acceptable, but I guess I have no choice. I'll make it brief and contact my colleague to inform my assistant.

Harper (*with a puzzled look*): Okay, take all the time you need, friend.

Fela (*with a sarcastic chuckle*): I'm sure we are not friends.

Harper (*stepping back*): Okay, that's just a figure of speech. I'll give you some space to make your call.

Fela: Thank you. I won't be long.

Harper exits the room. She was a nurse, so unruly patients are not new to her. But she is taken aback and annoyed by Fela's prickly attitude. She brought this stranger, a man, into her home with no hesitation. Despite the circumstances of the storm, she could have left him with the rest of his group. She had no need to extend her home and personal treatment to this man.

Dismissing her doubts, she decides to make some dinner for Fela for the evening. She hopes some food in his stomach and some more rest will turn him a little more pleasant. She grabs a pot to prepare homemade soup.

When Fela calls out for assistance, Harper returns to the living area.

Fela: Ms. Sun, I'm done.

Harper: You're done? Did you inform the people you needed to let know you are all right?

Fela: (*dry coughing*): Ye— yes.

Harper: Oh … let me grab you a glass of water and some more pain meds. *(Fela continues coughing as Harper retrieves the water and medication.)* Here you go.

Fela *(taking a big gulp*): Ah … thank you.

Harper: So here is my plan of action. I'm going to prepare some soup for you. I cannot fully cook any meat because it would take more time and energy. I'm operating on a generator with just enough fuel to last about three days.

Fela (*bowing his head in disappointment*): There's no possibility of me getting to a hospital?

Harper (*shaking her head*): Not tonight or tomorrow night, Z. You have basically expert care, and I can make you more comfortable. Consider this your hospital for now, Fela.

Fela (visibly frustrated): Okay … I'm not hungry. My head and ankle hurt. Here is the thing: You're not married. Your boyfriend, however, comes in, sees a black man with dreads on your sofa bed. Then what?

Harper (*smirking*): Ah yes, my boyfriend. He is here right now. Let me get him out of the bedroom upstairs.

She opens her bedroom door. Out comes Flurry, a rumbustious two-year-old husky. Harper gets the jumping dog settled and walks him down the wood stairs by his collar. She ushers Flurry to Fela to get a good sniff of the man. Fela is a little taken aback by the stout husky. Flurry sniffs, then licks his hand, but Fela does not want to pet him.

Harper: Okay, get back upstairs, Flurry. I'll be up there shortly.

Fela: Okay, got it. You live alone with Flurry the dog.

Harper: Yes.

Fela: Well, that's a little comforting.

Harper: Why do you seem so vigilant? Who is going to freak out if they see you, a black man, here?

Fela: Yes, that part. The fact is that this is the Canadian wilderness, miles away from civilization. No one will hear me scream if some mob comes up in here. You're a white woman in an expanded cabin. What are the optics here? But also, I am just as prejudiced of you as someone out there in the wild yonder. What if you screamed foul? That's all you must do, and that would be the story.

Harper (*mentally fading*): First, nobody is busting up in here, okay? I have a Glock 21, a Winchester rifle, and an old Mossberg. Second, none of my neighbors have pitchforks, a noose, or wear white sheets on their heads. I can guarantee that it is much safer here than down south, I'm sure. You don't like white people, do you?

Fela: Somewhat … white women especially.

Harper (laughing sarcastically): Wow! Now there is a bombshell for me tonight. Well … Z, for the next two nights, can you like me a little? I'm taking care of you, nothing more. We came to help you. There's no need to be hostile. You can be prejudiced when I get you back to Yellowknife. I'm going to need some respect and pleasantness from you, okay? We can get through this, and I'll get you where you need to be when the roads become passable. That's my promise.

Fela: I'm not a knuckleheaded, ignorant thug with no manners. I'm going to be professional. I'm educated and have wealth. I will compensate you for your service and housing once we get to town.

Harper: You don't get it. What did I just say about respect? Anyway, I'm going to leave you for now, as I need some rest myself. If you need something, there is a bell right here on the stand. Ring if you need me.

Fela: If you're offended, I—

Harper: Good night, Z. Remember to ring the bell if you need something.

Harper heads upstairs and retires for the night. She has been a little offended but not detruded. She understands from her former line of work that you deal with distressed people from all walks of life. Emergency-room patients can be rude and disorderly when they are in life-and- death situations and dealing with pain. She is mentally tough for what she endured with her ex-husband and the pandemic.

Her hope is that tomorrow, Fela will be in a better mood. Is he all right? He was concussed, after all, but his injuries are not life threatening. Maybe she should at least take him to Spen's cabin, where Jun and Barry are. She doesn't need this even though she is gravely lonely.

She lies down with Flurry by her bedside. Her Glock is reachable for the one percent chance of shenanigans with Fela.

Chapter 3

The next day has arrived. Harper is refreshed and ready to re-engage with her guest/patient, Fela. She feels uplifted to have him as company in her home. She is hoping to enfeeble his hostilities, prejudice, and smug bravado. She hurts, and she has this instinct that he is really hurting inside from something. His prejudice has manifested from somewhere in his life. Addressing it with him—over just a few days—is a long shot. She plans to start with a warm, hearty breakfast for him with his medicine.

Fela is awake and looking around, still frustrated as he was yesterday. Harper is behind the curtain in the tiny kitchen, mindful of her energy consumption. As she makes a breakfast feast for Fela, she jokingly calls him "Patient Z" in her head. When she opens the curtain, she reveals a tray with a plate of eggs over easy, ham, bacon, grits, and toast, along with his pain meds, water, and apple juice.

Fela's eyes widen at the sight and smell of the meal, but he does not reveal a smile of delight. He quickly goes back to a scowl. Harper sets everything up for Fela's easy access. She gives him a smile and a nod and says, "Enjoy. I'll be right back," before she grabs her food.

Fela takes small bites. His appetite has not returned, but he is overwhelmed by her effort. She returns to sit on a makeshift stool as she consumes only a bagel with some cream cheese.

Harper: How did you sleep, 2Z? How was your pain?

Fela: Sharp pains. I couldn't get comfortable. Harper: Why didn't you ring the bell or shout out for me?

Fela: There was nothing you could do. I got to sleep. It took me about two hours.

Harper: Are you still frustrated? Are you still uncomfortable with me?

Fela: Yes, and yes, but I will be respectfully patient.

Harper: Still not comforting, but wait I have a notification.

Fela: Anything good?

Harper: I have good news. We should be good to make a run to Yellowknife by noon Thursday.

Fela: That is great. Really? I know you're ready for me to be out of your hair.

Harper: You're not that bad, just need to let go of some things. I don't know why you have such animosity towards white women, and me for that matter. Want to talk about that?

Fela: Could you help me stand instead? I feel a bit of optimism.

Harper: I will walk you around a bit in the cabin if we can talk and share some of our hurt with each other.

Fela: So, you're a behavioral health specialist as well? Why would I share anything? We are strangers, and I'll be gone soon. Well, since you won't help me walk a bit, can I have a glass of whiskey?

Harper: Dude, you're on some heavy ibuprofen of the 800-milligram variety. I'm nursing you to good health, not cardiac arrest or a bleeding ulcer. You've been concussed. You should refrain from any alcohol for a while.

Fela *(rolling his eyes)*: You're the medical expert.

Harper: I was just a nurse.

Fela (*hesitating*): Why are you no longer a nurse? You weren't one of those angel-of-death nurses, were you?

Harper (*warmly laughing*): No! Not at all. That is the funniest thing you have said—well asked, anyway.

Fela: Well, in normal circumstances, I do have a sense of humor.

Harper (*getting serious*): No. I got burned-out from the rush.

Fela: The rush of what?

Harper: The pandemic, the people coming in and being rolled out in bags to the morgue. It became too taxing emotionally—hundreds of people, give or take, a lone. I was a trauma nurse, but because of the inflow of sick people and staff shortages, I moved ever y where, taking care of patients in the ICU on ventilators and life support. I lost count. Over a hundred people I took care of with COVID. I watched people die in front of my eyes. Two of them were good friends.

Fela (*with a compassionate expression*): Oh wow, that's terrible.

Harper: I wasn't alone in the fight. I had a loving husband to come home to in Yellowknife. At least that's what I thought. You see, Flip wanted to be an adventurer/adrenaline-junkie TV star. He had a following on Log Warrior Tube; it's big here in Canada. He got a massive following. I was in three of his videos, doing skydiving and wood-chopping challenges while taking shots. He ended up getting a deal in the United States before the pandemic hit hard up here.

Fela: I'm sorry.

Harper (*tearing up*): You don't want to know the why? Too damn bad. I'm going to tell you, anyway. It's not like you can run out of here while listening to me.

Fela: (*throwing his hands up as if in defeat*): Okay, Harper, what happened?

Harper: As I worked these shifts, he signed a contract all by fax, three years at $450,000 total. When he did that, the surge had just begun, people rushing into the hospital like a MASH unit. I was holding on. I thought I could transfer to a hospital down there in America. Hell, my husband has made it. I really could chill for a while once the pandemic was over.

Fela: But what?

Harper (*making a fist*): But what? … Exotic Wings, that's what happened. A floozy video vixen, twenty-two years old. While I'm going through the emotional ringer with this virus destroying lives, he manages to find love. You see, he initially flew down to Nevada for the first meeting. No contract was finalized, but he had her there in Sin City's gore of lust. He came back a different person. We were drifting apart. I thought it was for safety precautions; I catered to him. I slept on the couch, showered in the second bathroom, everything. I thought that was the reason he didn't touch me anymore and stopped saying he loved me.

Fela: Dang.

Harper: I'll wrap it up. He left right before the border between the states and Canada closed and moved in with her. I tried to plead with him. I even forgave him for the Vegas weekend escapade, but there was nothing I could do. I was hammered with the surge of patients. He still faxed me divorce papers from Las Vegas. I signed them; it was final. On top of that, I contracted COVID, but it wasn't bad for me. I was psychologically devastated by the hurt of Flip and the death around me more than by the physical illness for myself.

Fela: That's it? (*Harper, wiping her tears, stands up.*) Wait … I'm truly sorry. You have gone through so much, and still are going through it. I see the bottles in the cabinet; you're drinking your life away, it seems.

Harper: Did something penetrate your walls? You're relating to me?

Fela: My mom went through a similar heartbreak, except my father never married my mother. He abandoned us when I was just three years old. My mother was emotionally obliterated. She worked hard to support us; she was a hospital custodian. But she drank nearly every night. She then turned to drugs for a little while but did kick the drug habit eventually—however, not before so many years of taking her anger out on me with belts and fists. I was a mirror image of my father, and she basically hated me for a while. I still loved her dearly, like I do now. It was rough, though, Harper. However, she had kids other than me and people in her circle. You don't seem to have anyone besides Flurry. He doesn't f ix the void, now, does he?

There is a long pause.

Harper: No, he doesn't. He is not closure for me. You don't like me for what ethnicity I am, but you understand me. How does that work, Z?

Fela: It works because I'm a human sympathizing with another human. I don't disregard that just because of my prejudice toward white people. I never thought less of you, Harper, and everything just makes sense with you now.

Harper: What?

Fela: Your pain, the shelf full of whiskey, vodka, and shot glasses, like you're pouring it down daily. I see the pills … antidepressants, are they? What are you doing to yourself out here—self-pity?

Harper: First, what do you care? Second, yes, I've consumed alcohol, abused prescription pills for some time. I got help for that, but I haven't stopped drinking. I was discarded like nothing by someone I dedicated myself to with all my heart. I watched people die after this pandemic came; many of them I knew personally. I put a gun to my head and in my mouth more than once, and no one was here to wheel me off the ledge! Nothing but divine intervention and gun malfunctions. Again, what do you care? I pulled you in, took care of you, and you're a damn racist.

Fela: I deserve that, but what you're doing isn't going to go away. You need more help. I'm glad those guns malfunctioned, Harper. You have a big heart; that's obvious. I can't take back how I feel, nor will I. That's very personal.

Harper: Yes and you see nothing wrong with that, do you?

Fela: No. I can't change that, because it's just something you wouldn't understand. All that matters is that I appreciate the care you have provided me. I will compensate you for the medical care you gave me.

It's fair because if I was in the hospital, I would have a bill.

Harper: I don't want your money. I'm not a hospital. I don't do this for anyone out here. Only in a serious emergency will I do this, and I've never had one until now. It was just fate that intertwined us in the moment of the event.

Fela: How are you surviving? Is this cabin paid for? Are you going back to the medical field?

Harper: No, I'm not. I'm on assistance. I don't need your charity. I will always be a caregiver; that is who I am. So, your turn. What about you, Fela?

Fela: Okay. I'll just get another pillow to elevate my leg some more. That is my only issue that is troubling me.

Harper *(perturbed)*: That's your story. Damn it, here is your pillow!

Fela: Hey! Really, what is your glitch?

Harper: You are, Fela. You are extremely guarded, abrasive, and just cold. I'm better off outside. It would be much warmer.

Fela: Well, if that makes you feel better, then fine. I'm not walking on eggshells here for you. I am the injured one that's concussed, right?

Harper: What do you need right now so I can barricade myself in my bedroom for an hour or two?

Fela: Well, what I need is to get to Yellowknife, but I guess for now, some meds for my head, thank you.

Harper: Consider it done, Mr. Fela.

Fela: Wow. No more 2Z?

Harper: No! It's for your friends, and I'm not one of them, remember? Here is your medicine. Enjoy. Ring the bell after an hour, okay?

Harper retreats up to her bedroom. There, she f lings the door closed and is greeted by Flurry. Harper drifts off to sleep in tears, as does Fela on the sofa bed.

A few hours later, Harper and Fela both awaken to darkness. Only the glow of the fire gives light to the cabin. Fela has a sharp pain in his ankle. The cabin's front door is open, but the f ire is not staving off any of the bitter cold. Fela can't get up to see what is going on. He doesn't have to wait too long to find out, as Harper, bundled up, reenters the cabin, shivering. She hits a switch, and the light comes on, to her relief. As Fela and Harper catch each other's eyes, she walks over to him to explain her exit.

Harper: Good evening, Mr. Fela. We had a little scare. The generator ran out of fuel from my miscalculations. Thank God I had an extra fuel can in the shed.

Fela: We good for now?

Harper: Yes, we are good for one more day.

Fela: So, we good all the way to tomorrow night?

Harper: It will be close. I will turn the heat on high tomorrow morning. It should keep us crispy after the generator cuts off. It will be your last night tomorrow, anyways.

Fela: What about you after tomorrow?

Harper: Me? Ah, the same thing I have been doing since before you came along.

Fela: Oh, I see. Harper, there is something under me that's uncomfortable. It's poking the left side of my back.

Harper: Okay, I'm gonna need you to arch your torso up so I can see.

Fela: Here goes … ouch. Do you see it?

Harper *(sarcastically)*: Yes, I do. It's your terrible bedside manner. LOL, no, it's my massive photo album. Sorry, I'll put this away up top.

Fela: Can I look through some of your photos?

Harper *(taken aback)*: Wow, really? Why do you want to eyeball my photo album?

Fela: Oh, I understand if it's too personal. I just want to kill some time since I'm not going to get back to sleep soon.

Harper: Sure, here you go. I'll be back once I'm done prepping meals for tomorrow.

One hour later.

Harper: Are you tired yet? Oh my God, you seem to be in a deep trance from my photo album. Why?

Fela: Fascinating. Your pictures are enchanting and tell stories without words. This one photo album is like a biography, and I'm just halfway into it. Can you pop a seat next to me?

Harper: Okay. … Why, yes, I'm detail oriented, with chronologically capturing every phase of my life. I do this because of one of my parents, my father; I wasn't too familiar with him in my life. He died when I was twelve. His name was Harvey. He and a fellow hunting buddy were killed by a polar bear way up north in the tundra.

Fela: I'm sorry to hear that; my condolences to you. I know that can't be easy, for a young girl to lose her father.

Harper: Thank you. It hit my mother hard even though they were estranged for five years. It sent my mom into a spiral of alcohol, drugs, and years of rehab.

Fela (*pausing with empathy*): I can relate and have some experience with that, Harper. However, let's converse on some of the moments in your life.

Harper: Okay, what catches your eye?

Fela: Your high school years to start. Wow, you were quite the athlete and academic, I see. You ran track, played basketball, did weightlifting, and played volleyball? How did you pull all this off ? Impressive. You were also on the debate team from what I see here. Painting … dang, you were a female specimen with a great deal of brains.

Harper (*trying to be stone-faced*): That is nothing. I was trying to avoid my home life and the shame of my mother. Everything I did, she only went to about three events total out of four years and multiple sports. She didn't even understand anything I did academically.

Fela: Your college years seem the same. Did you get your degree?

Harper: No … I did two years. I took a hiatus; I went up to Yellowknife with some friends. One of them was entering the medical field, and she sold nursing to me. We stayed there for two weeks, and in that time, I met my future husband, Flip Boga. You know the rest from there.

Fela (*flipping through the album*): Okay, this is so much. I shouldn't try to finish this, but these photos you're in the hospital. You're curled up in your bed with IVs and monitors. Is it safe to say these are from when you contracted COVID, like you alluded to earlier?

Harper: Let me see. Oh no … Fela, not at all, sir.
Oh God, I forgot about this photo I had the nurse take of me. You see, me and Flip were expecting once, but I had a … miscarriage.

Harper becomes visibly uncomfortable and teary eyed at the mere mention of the word. Harper is a perfect iceberg with so much below the surface, as is Fela. At this point, Fela closes the photo album and hands it to her.

Fela: I get it. Here you go; I am sorry for triggering you. I got a little triggered because I have emotional pains, as you well know.

Harper: I sincerely appreciate you conflating our emotional instabilities and internal pains. So, will you feel for me more than as a caregiver after all of this is over? Will you share with me a little in these next twenty-four hours or so?

Fela: I embrace our little emotional interlocking, but whatever I may feel about you, the actions that happened years ago should drive my behavior now. To answer your question, I still don't think it really matters if I share with you. I will have deeper respect and appreciation for you, Harper, after it's done.

Harper (*with a disappointed expression*): Okay, I'm going to retire for the night. Are you going to be able to sleep?

Fela (*untruthfully*): Yes … good night, Harper.

Chapter 4

Fela has been laid up, staring at the log ceiling, pretty much all night, his pain being in the eight- out-of-ten range. However, that's not his deepest worry anymore. His worst worry has been psychological for the last twenty-four hours. He gives some contrition for the fact that he has refused to show Harper the openness she has shown to him. He is realizing that she is a unique, fascinating woman. Are his thoughts of her pure and innocent? Is he becoming attracted to her? He doesn't allow these thoughts to go further, as they betray his principles.

The same can be said of Harper. Is she fascinated by Fela out of a pure humanitarian need to nurse him to good health? Is she attached to Fela at this point? Loneliness is an obvious culprit; she dismisses it out loud, but subconsciously, the fascination is a mystery. So, she tells herself to stick to the business of keeping him comfortable—and getting him to Yellowknife by Thursday.

The day passes fast. The two find themselves cordial with each other. They share chuckles. Harper plays music for most of the afternoon hours. She dances. As her hair bounces all around, Fela cannot hold in his laughter. Even with his pain, the laughter tickles and numbs his body and his thoughts.

The sun has set and is far off; the clock strikes 10 p.m. Whitney's "I Have Nothing" is playing for a second time, the song blaring in Fela's eardrums. However, he does not complain; he sees Harper is focused on her feelings. He assumes she's thinking of Flip.

Harper wipes her eyes a bit. She turns to Fela to converse about tomorrow's actions.

Harper: Well, Fela, this is your last evening here in this cabin. I guess you got more than you bargained for in your Canadian experience. Are you happy?

Fela: Well, yes, I'll be happy to be in a warmer bed, my own back in Atlanta. I know you're relieved not to have to deal with this abrasive Negro. LOL.

Harper: Fela …

Fela: Bad joke, I'm sorry. We were on a roll with humor and feel-goods today.

Harper: Yes, feel-goods. … So how can I comfort you for your last night? You haven't been sleeping. I need you to sleep. I need you refreshed and ready. I'll do whatever it takes to achieve a level of comfort for you. I'm a former nurse, but still at heart, I'm on the job. Tell me what you need. I'm willing to grab my extra cot out in the shed. I can put it next to you and play ocean music for you—whatever it takes to soothe you.

Fela: Okay, okay, I know you have some sleep med with these high-dose pain meds. I know you have some type of sleep remedy. You worked in a hospital. You know doctors, surgeons. Hell, if you have propofol, I trust you to give it to me. I want to sleep; that's all. I don't need you next to me for that, just good meds.

Harper: LOL. I don't have propofol, nor would I give you that extreme. I know you've heard of Michael Jackson. I have some sleep med. It's not a prescription one; however, I know it will help you sleep tonight comfortably. If you don't need me here next to you, I understand. I'm here for you and whatever you need me to do to achieve the result of sleep. I'll be right back, okay?

Fela: No, never mind the meds. I'll be in a hospital tomorrow. I'll just take some warm tea, please.

Harper: Sure.

Harper heads to the kitchen to prepare some tea while Fela adjusts himself to get comfortable. She is disappointed and angry, pounding her fist into her palm. Tomorrow, she will be back in the groove of her lonely life.

Harper is deep in thought. She wants to have a drink later; she knows it will make the situation better but not healthier. Rational thoughts are nonexistent right now, in this moment. She is contemplating something kind of outrageous—something truly driven by the situation. She must do it; it's her only chance, so she must take it.

She finishes the warm, soothing cup of tea. She serves it to 2Z, retreats to the kitchen, and grabs a bottle of whiskey. Harper tells 2Z she will clean up and then be back in about thirty minutes to get the teacup.

2Z sips away in gratitude as he thinks deeply on their conversation as well as his actions with her this whole time. He is seemingly in a deep trance, and then he gets drowsy and drifts off for some minutes.

Harper: Everything okay? Fela?

Fela (*drowsy*): Yes … sorry I dozed off. I guess maybe I am sleepy after all. A little hard to keep my eyes open.

Harper: Go ahead, crash. You need rest. Do you need anything for extra comfort? Anything?

Fela (*dozing off*): No. I'll see you in the morning.

Harper pours her second drink and thinks hard for about fifteen minutes. She slams the glass on the floor, tired of running to alcohol. She darts off upstairs, reemerging minutes later in her robe.

She makes her way to the modified sofa bed area, where 2Z is resting. She begins to adjust and elevate his injured leg some more. The movement causes 2Z to open his eyes for a bit, but he is totally zoned out. Harper's eyes widen, in fear of 2Z's response, but he reaches his hand out to her. She takes his hand, clenches it tight. Her heart is racing with a pinch of excitement. 2Z is loopy. Holding her hand, he tugs at her as if he wants to pull her to him.

Harper has zero hesitation. She lies by him. She plants her head on his shoulder. She glides her hand across his arm. 2Z has the build of a track athlete, toned and chiseled. She likes what she is feeling. He brushes her hair gently with his left hand.

Fela (*opening one eye*): Harp … I don't think this is right. I don't think this is … wait.

Harper: Can we pretend it's right for about an hour or two? I just want to lay here with you. You say I'm your friend now, so do a friend a favor. You're leaving tomorrow and you'll forget all about this.

Fela (*seemingly high or drunk):* Ah … there is something you should know, my assistant. You know what? Never mind.

Harper: Cool, because your hand gliding through my hair feels wonderful.

2Z is still in a trancelike state. Harper gets looser. He seems to tug at her robe, unaware of his actions. She sits up, untying her robe front and flinging the robe on the floor, revealing some skimpy camouflage boy shorts, more like panties, with matching sports bra. Her tattooed, voluptuous frame curls up on his right side.

2Z, half-incoherent, glides his hands over her thighs, back, and shoulder. He can't process what's happening as he kisses her cheek a couple of times.

A tear rolls down Harper's face. She feels so desired, being in a man's arms again. She hasn't been intimate or had intercourse in over two years; she has been so bitter. She is cautious of 2Z's injured leg. She really wants him at this point, telling herself it's more than lust. Despite the solitude, despite his attitude, she sees so much love in him. She doesn't know why he is so angry with anyone in life.

He grabs the back of her neck, pulls her to his lips. Tongues come out to lock as one for this kiss, and then they kiss seemingly for an eternity. Harper agonizes over wanting to do more at this point, but he is in no condition. They break from their long kiss, and they rub noses. She purrs as she sweats. She begins to sob; in less than twenty-four hours, she will be alone again. Her tears are rolling. His hands whip them away one by one. However, his head goes back, and he drifts off again.

Harper won't wake him this time. She intertwines her right leg with his uninjured leg. She dozes off, and the two sleep until sunrise.

Seven hours later.

Harper: Are you happy since soon, you'll be away from me?

Fela (*looking sad*): Harper, what happened earlier, I—

Harper: It's okay. Please … I can't explain what came over me.

Fela (*puzzled*): What do you mean? I don't know if I was dreaming or sleepwalking. I think I groped you in some way. God, I think I did. We were laying together. I don't know if it was real or not.

Harper: It's okay. I'm not angry or appalled. I kind of made sure you did touch me. Well, I ensured you were a bit loopy to not really think anything of it. I … you know, we are pulling up to the emergency room entrance. Let's get you admitted, get some tests done. I'm sure I did everything so that nothing is infected.

Fela: Can you finish what you really want to say?

Harper: Let's get you in, okay?

Fela *(frustrated*): Okay. Can I use your phone so I can get my partner and assistant here by tonight?

Harper: Of course.

Fela is admitted to the hospital and scheduled to stay only a night. Harper was on point. Her outstanding nursing skills ensured Fela has no infections whatsoever; she treated his concussion properly. As he lies in the bed— antsy, ready to get back to Atlanta—Harper is still there with him until a very loud, older black man walks in along with a lanky, fancy black woman. They walk in like they own the hospital. Harper is taken aback by them, but she knows they are his business associates.

Fader: What's up! Man, it's good to see you! We were so worried, man.

Fela: Were you now?

Farisa (*planting a pecking kiss on Fela*): Hey, honey.

Fela: Hey, Farisa, I'm sorry.

Farisa: You should be. (She turns to Harper.) And who is she?

Harper: I'm Harper. I took care of your boss for the last couple of days.

Farisa: Bunny. I'm his fiancé—his fiancé. We are getting married—maybe a little sooner now, since I almost lost him.

Harper: Farisa, is it? I don't know what a bunny is. I told you what my name is, did I not?

Farisa (*with a sarcastic laugh*): That is what I said, isn't it?

Harper stares hard at 2Z.

Fela: Farisa, that's rude. Please, she has taken care of me so that I am here now, talking to you.
Come on, dear, there's no need for this type of attitude with her.

Farisa: Don't tell me how to react! You contacted Fader first, before me, because you were shacked up with Elisa all this time. Why didn't she get you to the hospital? Why didn't you insist?

Harper: I'm going to head home.

Fela (*looking very concerned*): No, please—

Harper: Y'all need to catch up.

Farisa: Good idea. Elisa, would you like forty dollars to get home to the woods?

Fela: Farisa, that's enough!

Fader: Farisa, that is so wrong, damn.

Farisa: What? You two fools wanted to keep me out of the loop. Why—because she is female? Was it something else? She doesn't look like she could nurse a Barbie doll.

Fela: Do you see my damn leg? What do you think was going on? I have had a concussion, a fractured ankle, and metal impaled into in my calf. Get over the ego, Farisa. I'm sorry, but I thought it was the right call.

Farisa: It's not enough. You could have died. We are not even married. Who would bury you?

Fader: Are you listening to yourself? Mama J would take care of it. She is the beneficiary, Farisa.

Farisa: Yes, and that's the problem, Fader and 2Z.

Fela: Fader, get a hotel room. You need some rest. I'm gonna call the nurse for some sleep meds so I can be ready to be discharged and fly out. Me and Farisa have some things to discuss.

Farisa: Oh, we can discuss whatever on the plane. I'm not sleeping here. I hope there is some sort of five-star accommodation here in yellow crap.

Fela (*utterly disgusted*): Wow … okay, Farisa. Y'all have a good night. I'm about to call in the nurse.

Chapter 5

Fader is totally disgusted by Farisa's actions but gives Fela a hug and tells him they will see him in the morning.

Fela doesn't request sleep meds after all. He was just very frustrated with his fiancé. He knows it was wrong to not inform her of his status, but he thought it wouldn't matter.

Fader and Farisa did bring Fela a new cell phone from Atlanta, so he calls his mother. They talk for twenty minutes, during which she lays down some revelations about Farisa. Overwhelmed by what has been revealed to him, Fela breaks down and sobs for about fifteen minutes straight.

Two hours later, he is still up, staring at the white ceiling, when he hears the hospital room door creak open. He feels enthused thinking it is Farisa coming to be with him.

Fela: I knew you weren't just going to leave me here—

Harper: I guess I couldn't now.

Fela *(shocked)*: What a surprise. You know visiting hours are over.

Harper: Come on now, 2Z. I worked here in this hospital. I know you weren't expecting to see me, but you're laying here alone.

Fela: Yeah, I know, right? Well, since you're here, let's chat it up. Are you going to finish telling me what you started to reveal in the car?

Harper: Right … well, I'm not too proud of this. But last night, I kind of roofied your tea with a little cocktail to relax you.

Fela: Why would you do that? Were you intentionally trying to harm me?

Harper: No! Not at all was that my intention for you, Fela. I just wanted to loosen you up so I could lay next to you—a moment of weakness. I started drinking. Then I thought about what you said about my alcohol dependency. I took two shots and got very emotional. Fela, I was just lonely. You were leaving. I just wanted to feel a man, just for an hour or so. Please don't be angry or want to press charges against me.

Fela stares into space. Harper paces for about five minutes before she says anything more.

Harper: Really? Fela, please say something.

Fela (*locking eyes with her*): I honestly can't find a reason to be angry. I'm flattered. Why the hell am I flattered?

Harper (*rubbing her eyes in surprise*): What? Okay, what sedatives have they given you?

Fela (*laughing*): None, I guess. In some ways, it all makes sense, but you could have any man.

Harper: That's not true, because I can't have a man like you.

Fela: Is it safe to say that the urges were just lust? I mean, you just wanted to lay with me. I remember bits and pieces of things. The mixture didn't make me so loopy that I remember nothing. I remember you undoing your robe, curling up on me; you were damn near nude. Was it just lust? If I didn't have injuries, would something sexual have happened?

Harper: That would be a … yes.

Fela (*blushing a bit*): I see. Have you ever been attracted to a black man, Harper? I mean, besides contact with them as patients in the emergency room, have you ever dated a black man? God, I hope Farisa is not around the corner listening to all this.

Harper (*laughing)*: You and I both know she is not here in this hospital. To answer your question, no, I haven't been with or been attracted to a black man. However, that's not by racial prejudice, just the fact that I was married and never thought outside the box. I was never attracted to a black man until about three days ago. I decided to go outside the box. That's why I loosened you up. Yes, I laid on you in my undergarments, and I took your hand so you could feel me.

Fela (*heart starting to pound*): Yeah, I remember that part vividly.

Harper: Are you not attracted to me at all? Did you not like anything I presented to your eyes? You don't like my body? Be honest. If you were not injured, under normal circumstances, would I be worthy of your kisses, your touches, sex, any intimate action?

Fela: Okay, hold up. First, your body is fantastic. You have some very lovely boobs, and the tattoos. It's a perfect number-10 combo.

Harper *(chuckling)*: Wow … okay, I accept that as a wonderful compliment.

Fela: Okay, since I hadn't touched a white woman in any way prior to meeting you. You took my hand to touch you. Your skin is very soft, smooth. It's safe to say I would be aroused by your flesh. It's safe to say I would under normal conditions. In that moment, we were that close. I, Fela Zamore, would bless your gardens with all of me. I'm saying this as an engaged man that loves his fiancé, Harper. It's just that simple, my friend.

Harper (*palming her mouth*): OMG, you said *friend.* That's a turnaround.

Fela: Can you help me stand up?

Harper: Sure.

She helps Fela up, as he wants to stand and stretch his legs. He hops around a bit, with Harper being his crunch.

It's four in the morning. Neither of them shows any signs of being fatigued. Harper has always been at ease with him from the time he was put on her sled. Fela has this overwhelming guilt about his prejudice and mistrust of her race. He decides he wants to tell her why. So, he sits back on the bed and asks her to sit next to him to listen.

Fela (*patting the bed*): Come sit here.

Harper: Okay.

Fela: One last thing that's very important that you need to know about me. So, about sixteen years ago, it was me and my older brother. Zedai was visiting a friend. His name was Jace—a white kid that was cool with Zedai. He lived in Peachtree City, about thirty-one miles from Atlanta. We drove down there in our mom's car. She didn't have to work, and she wanted us to get out of the house. Now, Peachtree City is very heavily populated, a white, wealthy, golf-type community. We stopped at this gas station to get some gas and grab a snack. We were leaving the store when this one white woman, Susan Deerdone, bumped into Zedai. Zedai was very polite. He attempted to apologize to her. Well, before I continue, are you good, Harper?

Harper: Yes, friend. Please keep going. I want to know.

Fela: Of course. Zedai said, "Excuse me, I'm sorry." She replied, "You are sorry." We shook it off, got in the car. We headed down the street getting to Jace's house and stopped at a red light. I looked to my right, and there was Susan Deerdone shouting at us while she was on the phone. The light turned green. Zedai hit the accelerator. So did she, and then came behind us, flashing lights. Two police cars were behind us. I told Zedai, "Pull over now." He didn't want to, but we had no choice but to stop and obey the instructions. I tell you four off icers came out. I'll never forget Off icer Berman came out with gun drawn on Zedai. No way was this police procedure by any stretch. Susan, being a white woman, got these off icers sicked on us like pit bulls. We didn't know what we did wrong. I was on the passenger side. One off icer had a gun on me. Damn, this is so hard, Harper.

Harper: Then don't tell … it's not that important to me if it is something that traumatic to you.

Fela: (eyes tearing up): No, you need to know the officer had the gun on me. He ordered me to get out. I mouthed off, protesting, "What did we do?" He yanked the door open, started dragging me out. Zedai's older- brother instincts kicked in. To protect me, he lunged for me. Officer Berman fired three shots, the fatal one striking Zedai in the neck. He was dead. I screamed as I was thrown to the concrete. I was put in the squad car, handcuffed for at least thirty minutes. I was given no explanation of what we were accused of doing. My brother stayed slumped in that car for the entire thirty minutes. Finally, another car came with a sergeant to explain to me that Susan accused my brother of taking her wallet while violently bumping into her. Her account was we knocked her down and the gas station clerk witnessed it.

Harper: Oh God … I need to hold your hand on this. It's a little overwhelming.

Fela: I'm almost done. Well, this went to court.

We didn't have money, but a kind soul, a well-renowned civil rights attorney, came to our aid because it was discovered that Susan falsified her statement to the police. Susan handed her wallet to the store clerk, who was affiliated with a white supremacy group. He later confessed to being aware that Susan handed it to him to go pursue us. When the smoke cleared, we filed a wrongful-death lawsuit, which we won, and were awarded ten million dollars. My mom retired. I went to Georgia Tech and got my degree in software development. Me and Fader put our heads together, formed TEXFRET Software. The thing is I still see Susan Deer done in my nightmares to this day. I've been in counseling off and on for years, trying to find closure for my brother.

Harper: What did she look like, Fela? Did she look like me?

Fela: About five-foot-five, same hair, early thirties.

Harper: Like me?

Fela: Yes, quite like you, Harper. She just wasn't as you.

Harper: It all makes sense now.

Fela: Somewhat, yes, but I realized that maybe in some abstract way, this has come full circle. Maybe this is a path to closure—to overcome my fears, to vanquish my demons, to finally put her in the wind, out of my thoughts and nightmares.

Harper: Where does this leave me? Who am I to you? Am I your friend or a demon that needs to be extinguished?

Fela (*squeezing her hand a little tighter*): You are my friend, Harper Sun—a special friend.

Harper: One more question; it is very important to me. Friends could love each other, so could you see yourself loving me more than a friend?

Fela: I …

Harper: You don't have to answer that. I am satisfied that I got you here—that you're alive to go back to Atlanta and to be able to walk down the aisle.

Fela's phone chimes.

Fela: Thank you. This text message is from Fader.
He is on his way, but Farisa is going straight to the jet.

Harper: That's my cue, then. We just need to formulate this goodbye.

Fela: Yeah, it is a little strange. We got a little too attached to each other.

Harper: You take care. I left my number and email on that notepad. All I ask is when you get back, situated with your daily business, please ring me up.

Fela: I will. Okay, you take care, and try to find some closure for yourself. You really don't need to be out in the woods like that, alone.

The two shake hands, and then Harper turns to walk out the door. Fela is conflicted. He really doesn't want her to leave. They have touched each other's hearts in so many ways. His eyes are already teary from telling her of his ordeal with his older brother. He doesn't know if he should be joyous to be leaving Northern Canada and getting back to Atlanta. He just stands there, no crutch, staring at the door.

Chapter 6

Four months later.

Friday evening in Atlanta at a live wrestling event, Fela and Fader are in VIP chairs next to the commentators. They are enjoying a no-holds-barred championship match featuring their wrestler. They are endorsing Evo Kry. The crowd is screaming, watching chair shots, blood, and chaos. Evo Kry versus Fu Wista is giving the crowd what they want in a wrestling match.

Thirty minutes later, the match concludes. Evo pins Fu Wista and wins the DSK championship belt. Fader and Fela are hysterical. They begin to head to the VIP locker rooms in the back.

Fader: All right, that's what's up! Our homey got the belt, Z.

Fela: Man, you already knew he was going to get it. Now, we can market him as the DSK champion. We can put that on the game cover and kill them on sales. I'm excited, man. Evo, that's the truth.

Evo (*busting in the door*): My dudes! We did it, ayo!

Fela: Yessir, my man. Congrats. I already knew they was putting it on you! You are good, though? Man, you took some crazy chair shots and flipping everywhere.

Evo (*laughing*): I'm good. It's all business. I hope y'all enjoyed.

Fader: We enjoyed, man.

Evo: Where do we go from here?

Fela: Wherever you want to grab something to eat— go find a lounge to smoke a cigar and toast. How that sound, champ?

Evo: Okay, man. I'll go take a long shower. They want to do a championship photo shoot with me cleaned, holding the DSK belt. That cool?

Fader: Yeah.

Fela: It's your world, brother. Yes, that's fine.

Evo: As a matter of fact, I'm gonna do a fifteen- minute shower and get this damn photo shoot done so we can drink and blow smoke. How does that sound?

Fader: It's fine with me.

Fela: Yeah, that cigar. The lounge is perfect. I'm trying to get home at one at least.

Evo: Oh yeah, how's the ankle? Man, I freaked out when I heard what happened, Z.

Fela: Thanks, man. Yeah, I'm trying to get rid of the limp. I want to start running by next month or so.

Evo: Good blessings there. I'll get this done as quickly as possible, y'all.

Fela receives a notification on his phone.

Fela: What is this? I got a missed call and a text message. Oh, dear … hey, Fader. Man, I'm gonna step outside to the parking lot and return this call.

Fader: Everything all right?

Fela: Yeah, I'll be out there. *(Fela doesn't get a chance to check the message because the phone rings again with an incoming call. He suddenly recognizes the number. It is an "oh shit" moment indeed as he realizes it's Harper.)* Yes … OMG, Harper, what's wrong?

Harper: Wow … you really wrote me off like a check, huh?

Fela: Harper? Oh God, dear, I'm so sorry. I know I haven't contacted you.

Harper: Oh, you have amnesia? You're blaming that on the concussion?

Fela: Okay, I'm not following here. This is the first time I've heard your voice in four months.

Harper: Heard my voice, yes … but you had a lot to say in your email. Are you going to deny that?

Fela: Yes, I have been working on recovery, a gaming console, and an energy drink launch. I couldn't have emailed you. What was the nature of this email?

Harper: Very hurtful, degrading. And to think I believed we connected … why?

Fela: That's a good question because I don't know about the email. What did it say, Harper?

Harper: I'll just tell you the good parts: "Thank you for your servitude. I finally got some vengeance on a white woman devil. You waited on me like a slave, and I savored every minute of it, snow bunny. Now, here are forty dollars. Enjoy your life in the woods. You never meant anything to me." Is this +

Fela: What's the date of that email?

Harper: April 14. Why? You already know this!

Fela: Yeah, it came from my email address—written by

Farisa: I take it. I broke up with her and fired her early April.

Harper: Really? Really?

Fela: Yes. She opened loans and credit cards using my name, and a shady business. She tried to manipulate my attorney to get my mother to up the amount on my life insurance policy. This was at the time I was laid up in your cabin with you nursing me. I was just a meal ticket to her; that's all it ever was from the beginning. You see, she is a shady, vindictive soul, and she wanted to hurt me by attacking you. Harper, she put some CIA bug-type device in the room when she left for the night. She heard everything we talked about that morning … everything.

Harper: Are you serious? She is that crazy, unstable, and maniacal? Are you serious?

Fela: Yes, Harper, that serious. My mom, Fader, and the private investigator I hired confirmed it.

Harper: Oh, Z, I'm sorry. I really am. However, it doesn't let you off the hook for not contacting me for all this time.

Fela: I lost your info on that sticky pad in the jet.

I went back, looked, and checked with the cleaning crew. Farisa must have found it or taken it out of my pocket while I was sleeping on the way back. Wait … your words are a little slurry, Harper. Damn, you been drinking, haven't you?

Harper: I needed to get the fuel for my anger to let you know how hurt and disrespected I felt.

Fela: Well, I didn't send it but still no excuse for your doing it now. What about finding closure?

Harper: Well, you found yours; that matters a lot to me. Fela, for the record, this was my first drink in four months.

Fela: I don't get it. Why?

Harper: I don't get it myself. Your circle is complete, not mine. It's still a big picture that you don't see, even after parting ways with Farisa. Did anything in that breakup have a little to do with me? Maybe you felt something for me? Never mind. This was a bad idea. I regret that I picked up the bottle or picked up the phone. We are good. I'm not going to call you anymore. I heard your voice, and you're doing well.

Fela: Wait, we don't need to part like this, Harper.

Harper: That's true, but honestly, I'm not a big phone chatter, Fela. Continue to do right by me and take care of yourself.

Fela: So, you're going to go back to that playbook?

Harper: I don't know how to deal with these feelings. Just call me back Friday. I should be better then; I am sorry for snapping. I hope to hear from you then. Bye.

Fela: Whatever you wish. Bye, Harper.

He knows what to do and where to be and who needs him—Friday afternoon in Northern Canada, Harper is returning from a trip to Yellowknife.

As Harper pulls up to her porch, a large bouquet of roses and a pillow shaped like a sun await her. Totally taken by surprise, she picks up the note attached and looks around, puzzled by the mysterious gifts. The note has a black heart drawn on it and says, "You are a Northern breath of beautiful air." She blushes.

An SUV comes down the path and stops alongside her jeep. Out of the driver's side pops Fela.

Harper *(blushing)*: OMG, I thought I said to call me, 2Z. OMG, what are you doing here?

Fela: You did say call, but the way you got off the phone worried me. You sounded hurt, and I'm tired of you being hurt. You've had a lifetime of it; I hope to change that maybe.

Harper: About that phone call—I guess I'm not sorry about it. I wanted you to feel bad. You mean more to me than you really can grasp, and I was just pissed off that you haven't realized it. We are friends, but from my perspective, we are not good friends, because you don't live here. We can't catch up over drinks every Friday and throw darts.

Fela: Harper, from the moment I left the hospital until I arrived back in Atlanta, I thought about you. I worried about you. I've gone to sleep thinking about you. I've dreamed about you, and I thought to myself, Was I wrong to think of you? Even before I cut sling with Farisa, and we were trying to plan a wedding, I thought of you. So, I decided to be very busy with gaming, endorsements, and wrestling investment, just to forget you. When it finally started to work, fate came in, and you called me just a couple of days ago. So, therefore, I'm here. I sent you the roses and stuffed sun thingy.

Harper: So, what are you saying?

Fela: Do you still want to fall in love with me?

Harper: No. I'm already there, Fela. If you're not there yet, I'm patient enough to let you catch up. However, there is no turning back for me, so if you want this, I'm here. Let me know right now.

Fela (*pulling her into his arms*): I'm there. I'm so there, Harper Sun. Can I convince you to come back to Atlanta with me? I want to take care of you. You want to get back into nursing? I know doctors. I can buy a clinic for you and supply doctors. Oh, and of course, Flurry—a nice big yard and doghouse for him. I'll give you what you want. But most of all, Harper, I want to give you me, and I want every bit of your beautiful soul. You're one-of-a-kind special. You're not a demon, sweetness. You were my angel that looked over my biased soul. What do you say?

Harper: Yes, to all of it, but the cabin is warm and cozy. Will you be all right to stay here tonight?

Fela: Yes, I have an overnight bag. So, want to giggle and toss darts?

Harper: Ah, no … I would prefer other activities on that sofa bed involving you and me. You like that idea better?

Fela: For sure. … Now come here and into my arms, where you should be.

THE END

Printed by Libri Plureos GmbH in Hamburg,
Germany